S0-BOJ-363

DISCARD

DEMCO

ABDO Publishing Company is the exclusive school and library distributor of Rabbit Ears Books.

Library bound edition 2005.

Copyright © 1995 Rabbit Ears Entertainment, LLC.,
S. Norwalk, Connecticut.

Library of Congress Cataloging-in-Publication Data

Kessler, Brad.
  The firebird / written by Brad Kessler ; illustrated by Robert Van Nutt.
      p. cm.
  "Rabbit Ears books."
  Summary: With the aid of his magical Horse of Power, a young archer fulfills the
increasingly difficult requests of Tsar Ivan and wins the hand of Princess Vasilissa.
  ISBN 1-59679-224-8
  [1. Fairy tales. 2. Folklore—Russia.] I. Van Nutt, Robert, ill. II. Zhar-ptitsa. English. III.
Title.

PZ8.K47Fi 2005
398.2'0947'02—dc22
[E]

                                                                    2004059645

All Rabbit Ears books are reinforced library binding
and manufactured in the United States of America.

ABDO
Publishing Company

THE FIREBIRD

ЖАРПТИЦА

written by Brad Kessler
illustrated by Robert Van Nutt

Rabbit Ears Books

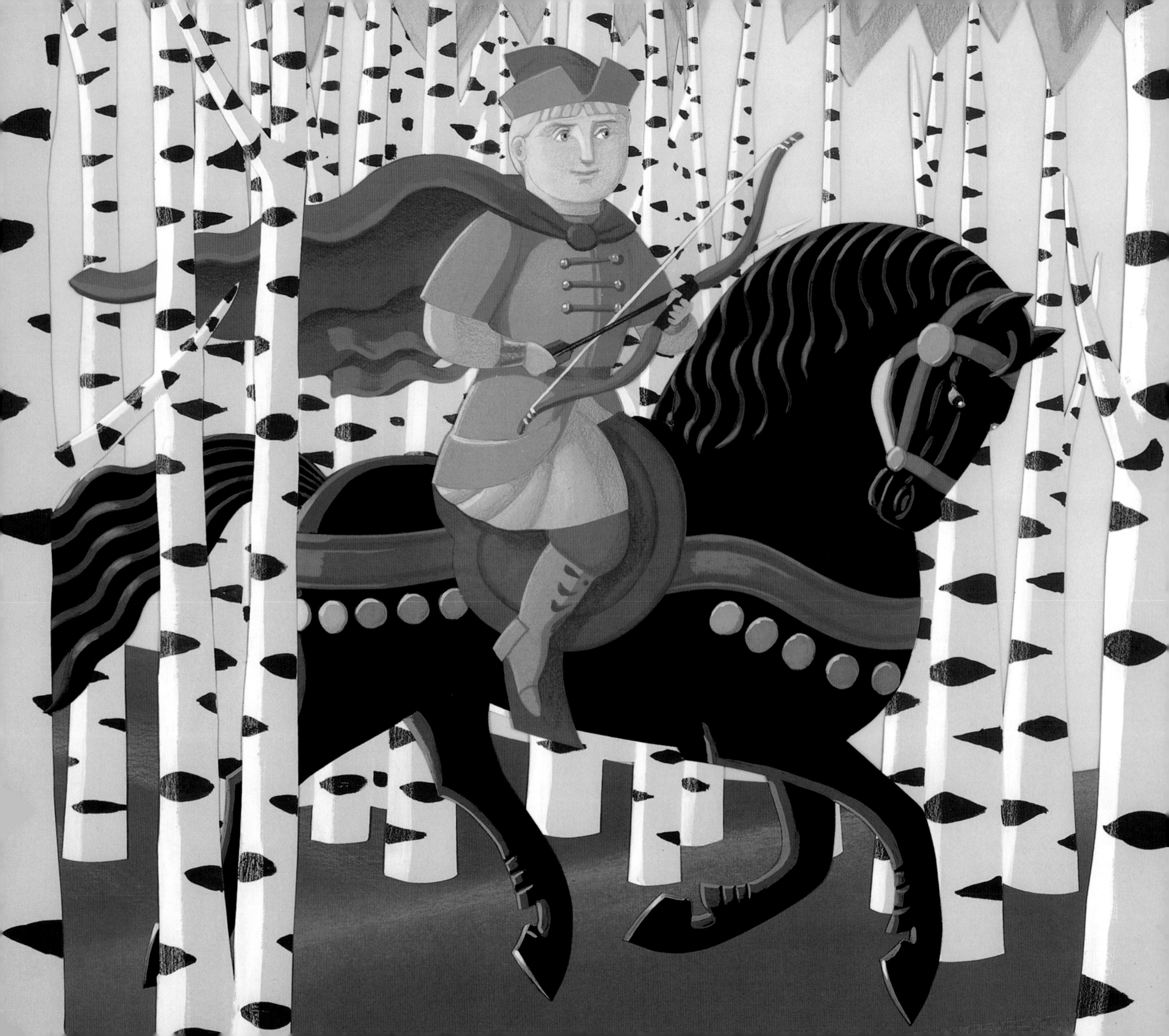

Along, long time ago in a certain kingdom in a certain corner of Russia, there lived a young archer who served in the czar's army. His name was Ivan and he rode a strong and wise horse—a Horse of Power—such as they had back in Russia in those days. The horse had iron hooves and eyes of fire and a mane of magnificent hair, blacker than the Baltic night. And Ivan and his Horse of Power were quite inseparable.

Now it came to pass that one day Ivan was riding his horse through the forest, and just as they were trotting along, the horse reared backward, startled by something on the path. There on a bed of pine needles lay a delicate golden feather, so brilliant that it glowed and was blinding to behold. Now such a feather could only belong to the Firebird, the rarest of birds in all of Russia.

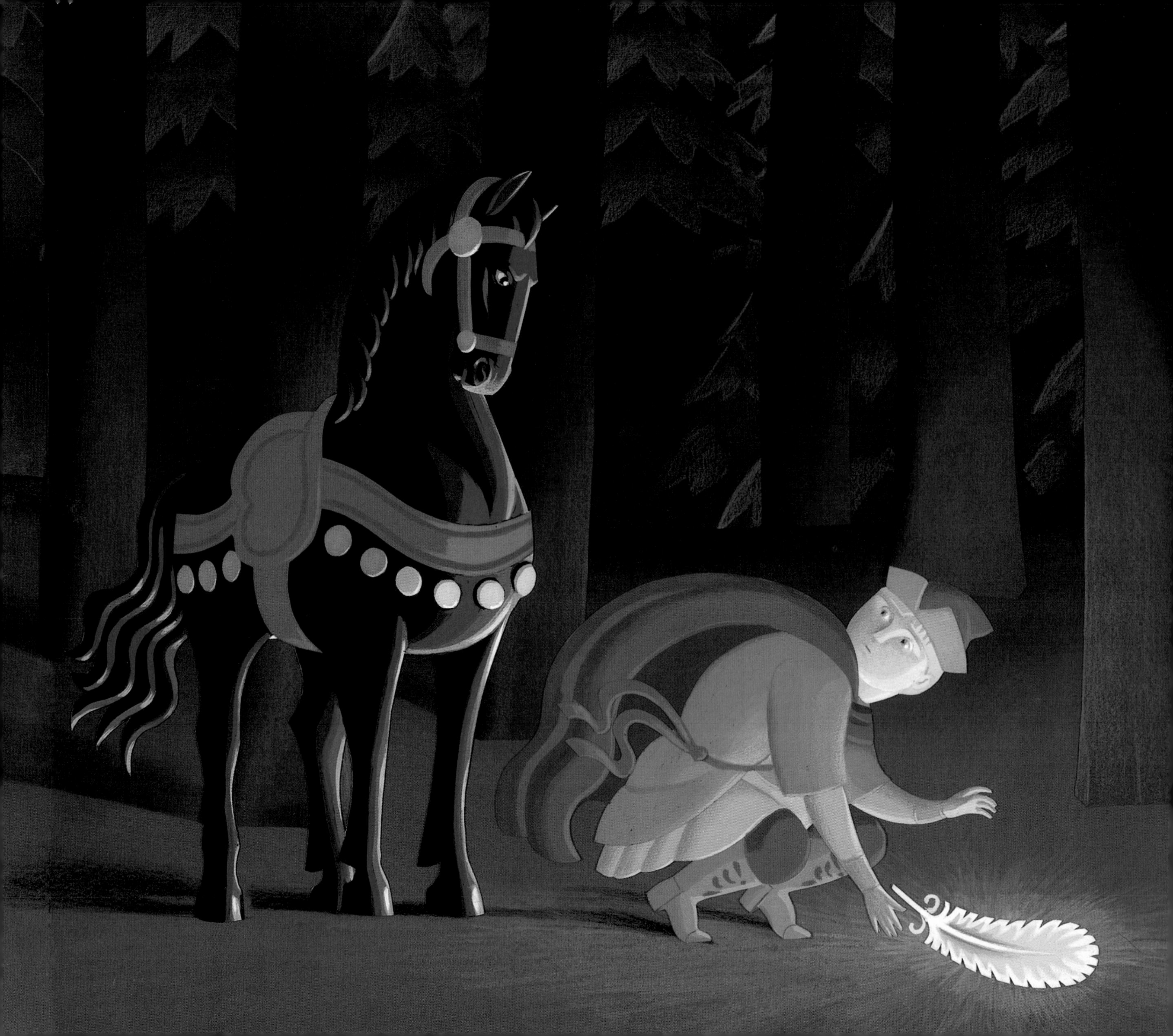

"Horse of mine, what luck!" Ivan yelled. "I will take this Firebird feather to the czar, who will surely repay me with kindness and gifts."

The Horse of Power, however, knew better. "Ivan," he said, "be forewarned. If you take this feather from the forest, you will most certainly learn the meaning of fear."

Now Ivan, who was as brave as the Russian winter is long, had no use for the meaning of fear. But as he held the feather in his hand, turning it this way and that, he thought of how pleased the czar would be to receive such a splendid tribute, and what types of gifts he might give Ivan in gratitude. So he ignored the advice of his horse and, taking the feather with him, rode through the forest to the czar's palace.

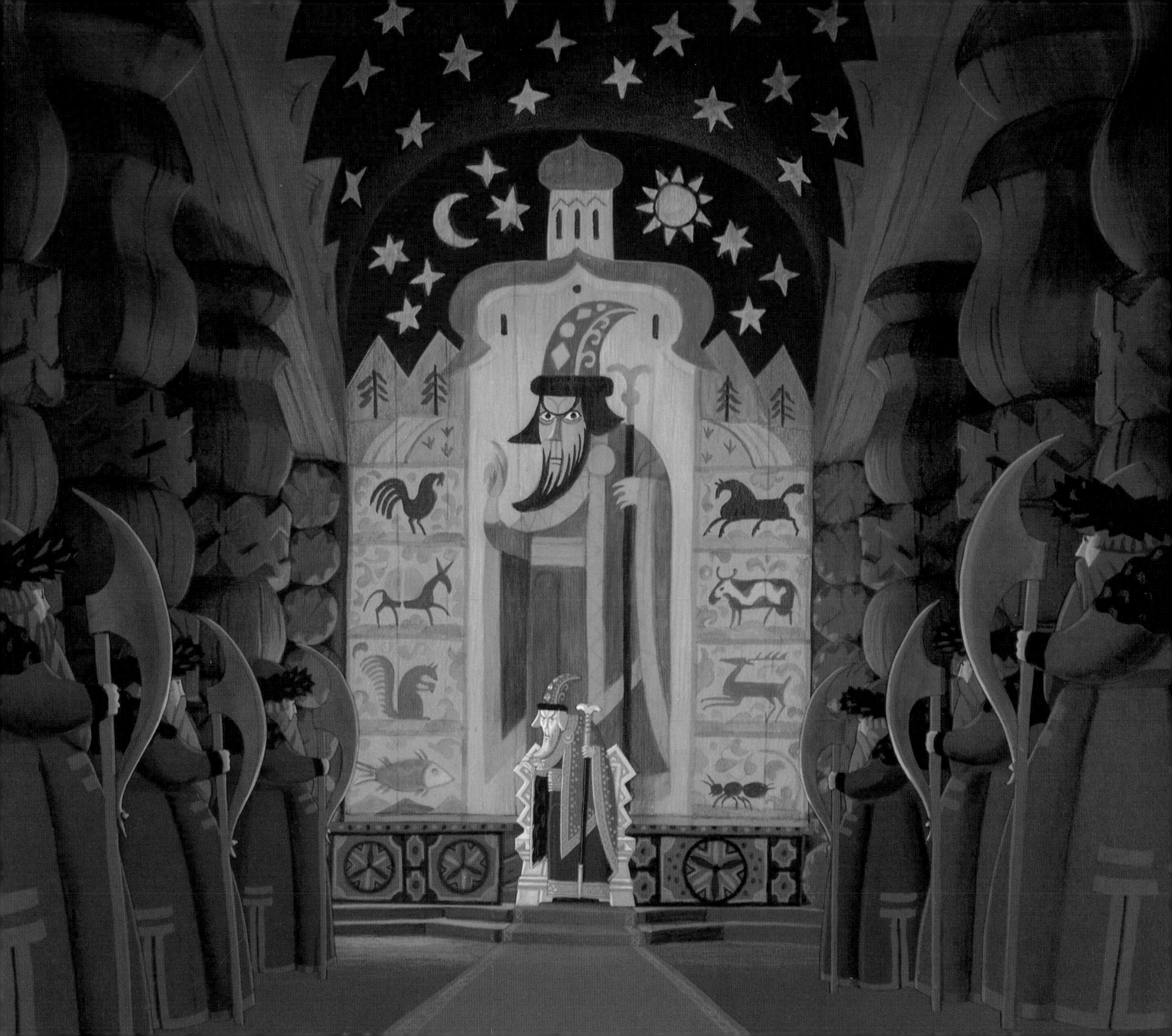

 Now the czar of this kingdom, let it be said, was not an especially pleasant man. He was an old and fearsome czar, who owned all the fields and lakes and mountains and trees and flowers. He owned all the animals and the birds and the fishes and the insects, too. He even claimed to own the stars themselves—and he threatened to punish people for looking at them without his permission. So vast was the czar's greed that he always wanted something more, and the people grew to fear his boundless cravings.

Yet Ivan was not afraid of the czar and he went straight into the palace and bowed before him. "O Great Czar," he said, "I have brought you a feather from the Firebird as a gift."

The czar took the feather, and a smile creased the old man's face. Then he looked down at Ivan and frowned. "Young archer," he sneered, "why have you brought me only the feather of the Firebird? A feather is surely not a fit gift for a czar. Bring me the bird itself, alive, or I will have you locked up in chains!"

You can imagine how shocked Ivan was at this, for not even the most skillful of hunters in all of Russia could capture the Firebird.

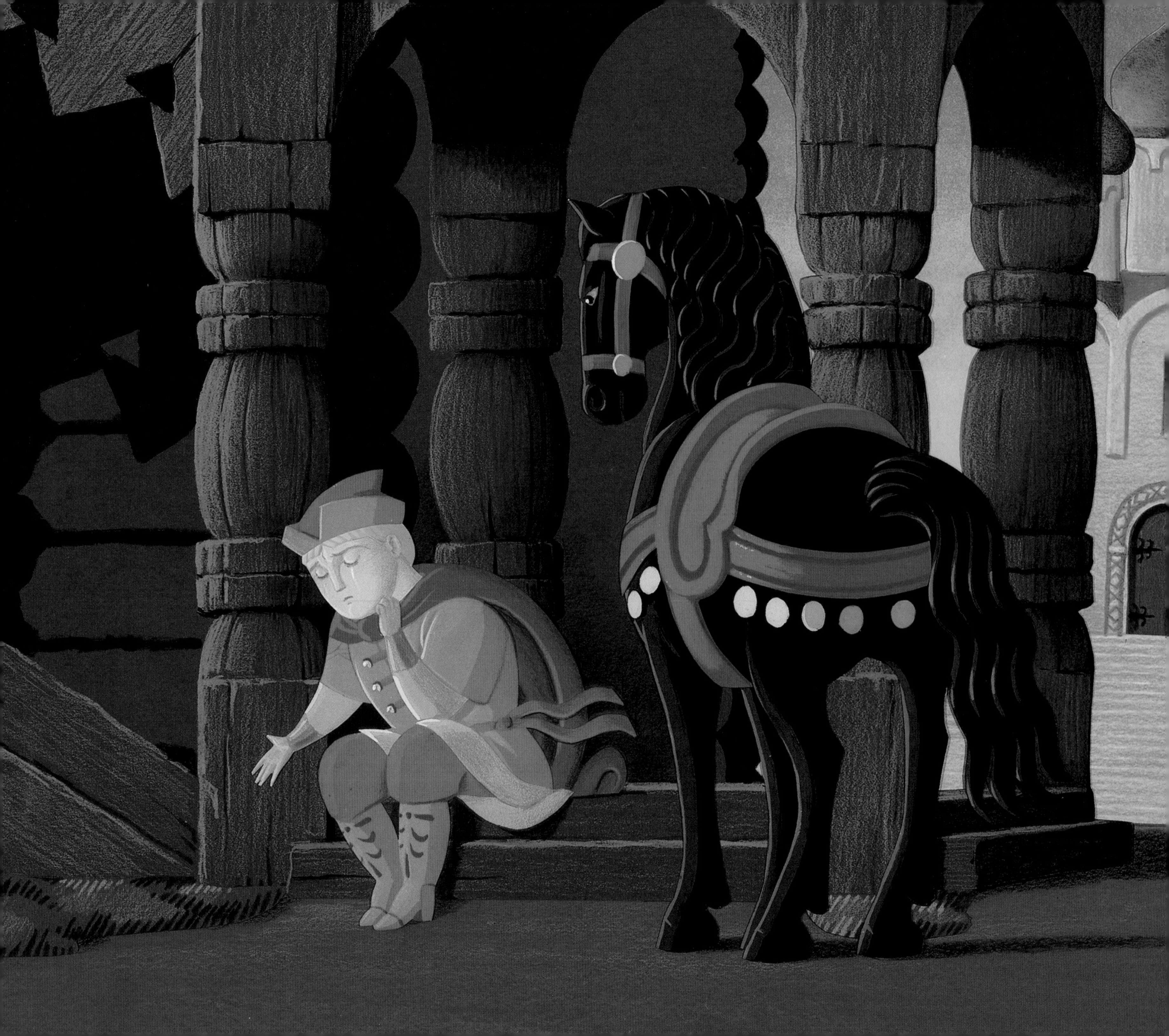

So Ivan bowed again and walked from the palace to where his horse waited. And there he cried softly to himself.

"Ivan," his Horse of Power asked after a while, "why are you weeping?"

Ivan told him what the czar had commanded, and then the horse spoke up. "I warned you if you took that feather you would know the meaning of fear, and now you do.

"Go back to the czar and tell him you will capture the Firebird, but first you require one hundred sacks of corn and another fifty of buckwheat groats."

So Ivan did as his horse said, and that night they scattered corn and wheat over an empty meadow.

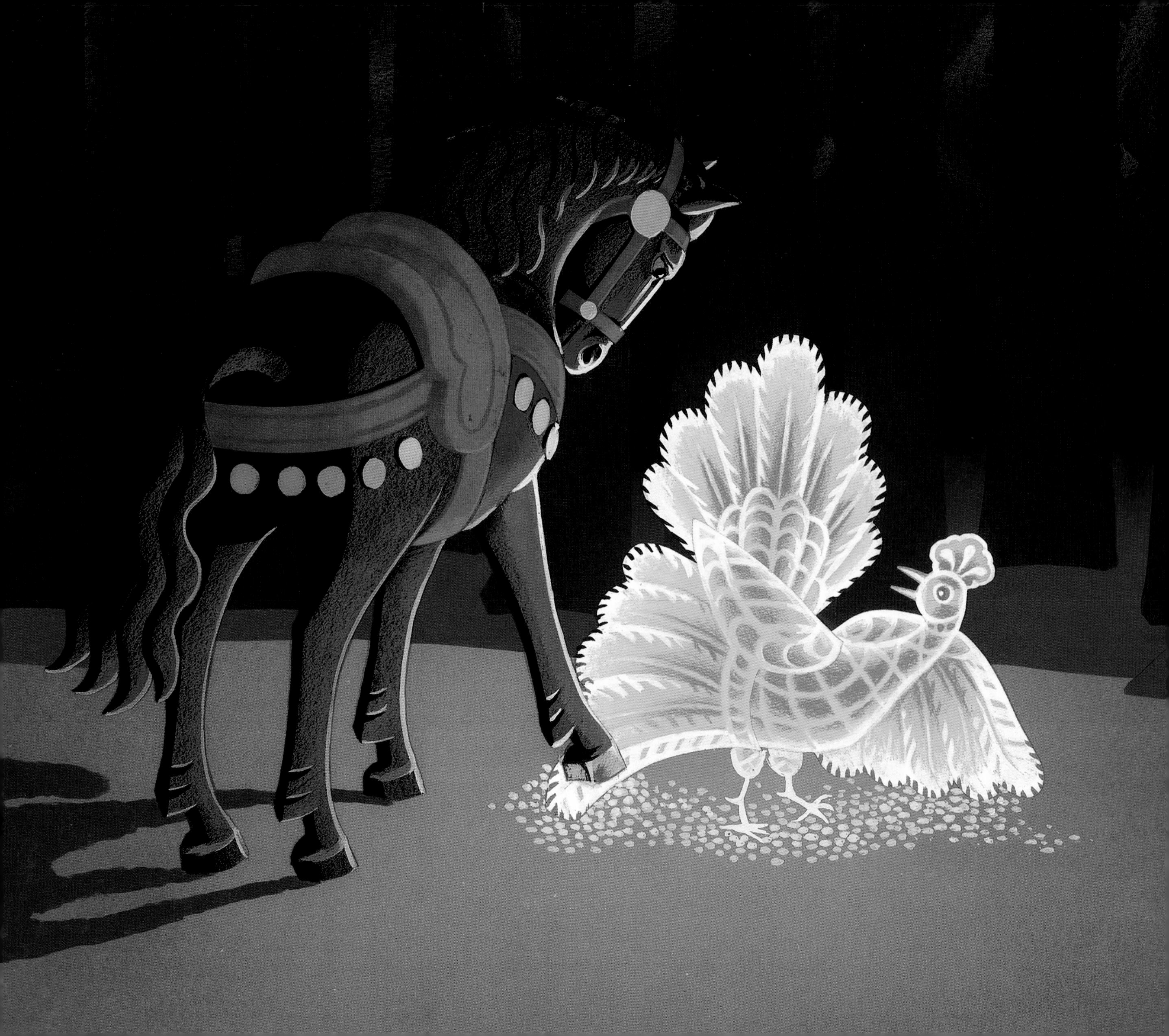

The next morning, as the sun slid over the forest, Ivan hid behind a tree.
Soon every bird and animal from all over the kingdom gathered there
to feast on the grain. And before long, a great wind blew from the north and
the birch trees bent backward and the blackbirds stopped their singing and
the Firebird, the great golden creature, spreading sparks from her gilded
wings, flew down onto the field and she, too, began to eat.

Meanwhile the Horse of Power
pretended to graze like all the other
animals, but slowly made his way
ever closer to the Firebird. And when
he was near enough, he pressed an
iron hoof firmly on the Firebird's
wing, pinning down the struggling
creature.

Ivan then sprang from the tree,
bound the bird's feet, and with her
rode off to the czar's palace.

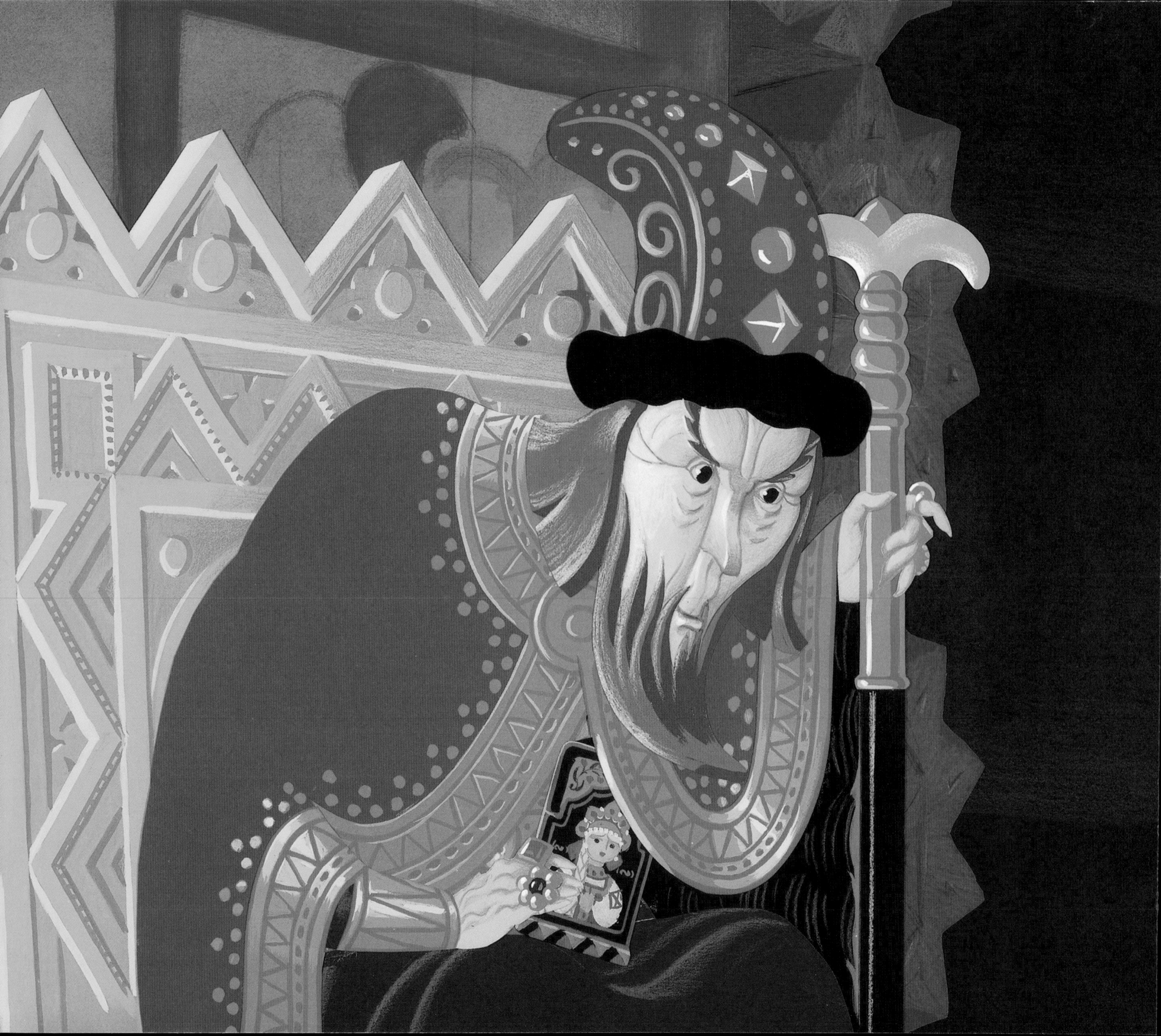

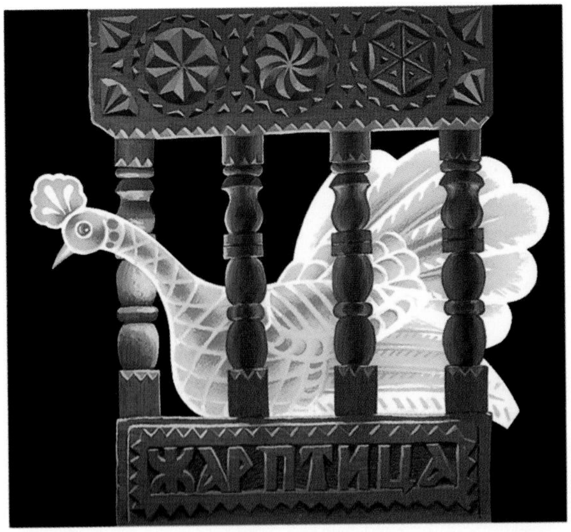
ЖАРПТИЦА

When he got there, Ivan triumphantly placed the Firebird at the foot of the czar's throne. And the czar was especially pleased, for since the beginning of time, no one, not even a czar, had possessed the Firebird. So he promptly ordered the bird locked in a large wooden cage. Then he turned his eyes upon Ivan.

"Young archer," he said, "seeing how skillful you were at trapping the Firebird, you will surely be able to bring me the bride I most desire: Princess Vasilisa. She lives in the Land of Never at the edge of the world. Bring her back and I shall reward you graciously. But if you fail, I will have you hung from your heels and beaten with whips!"

So Ivan made his way back to where his horse waited. And there he wept more bitterly than the time before, for the czar's request was quite impossible, as no one had ever been to the Land of Never, where the sun rises from a sea of flames.

After a while his horse spoke up. "Ivan, I warned you if you took that feather you'd have to live with the consequences. Now go to the czar and ask for a silver tent with a gold roof and all manner of fine foods to offer the princess. Then we shall be off."

Ivan did so, and with a silver tent embroidered in gold and leather sacks filled with the finest of foods, Ivan and his Horse of Power lit off for the Land of Never at the edge of the world.

It is a long journey to the Land of Never, and there are no maps to get you there. They rode on, day and night, through thick forests and empty meadows, over vast cold plains of arctic tundra. And finally one morning, after weeks and weeks, they came to the Land of Never at the edge of the world, just as the red sun was rising from its sea of flames.

Ivan peered out into the sea of flames, and there, in a small pocket of water between two fiery swells, Princess Vasilisa rowed a tiny silver boat with golden oars. And Ivan straight away was quite smitten with love for the wonderful princess.

So he set up the silver tent and took out the dishes of fine food: eggs from fishes bred in tidal pools of champagne, sausages made from milk-fed doves, chocolates so sweet and rich they could feed a family for an entire year.

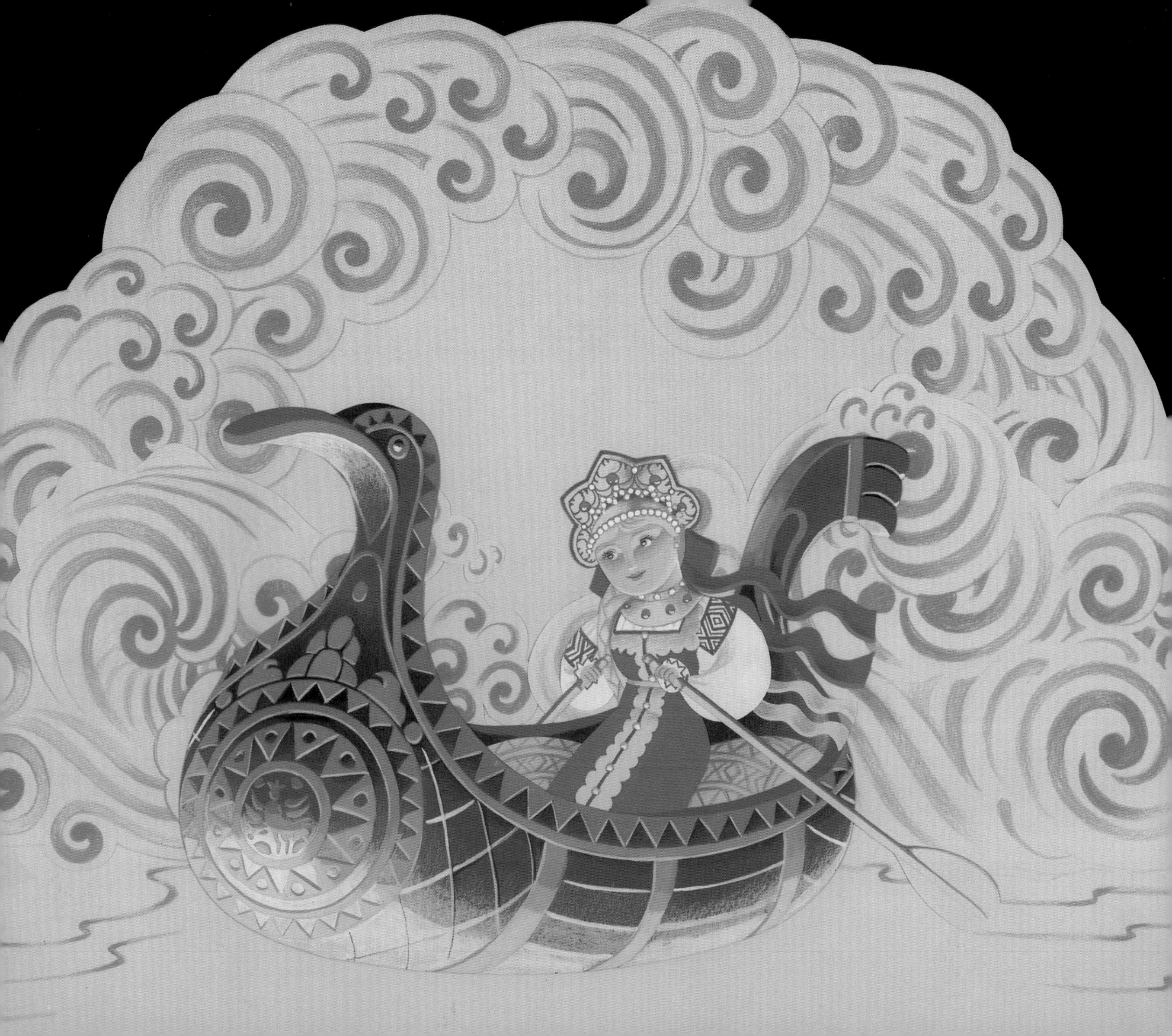

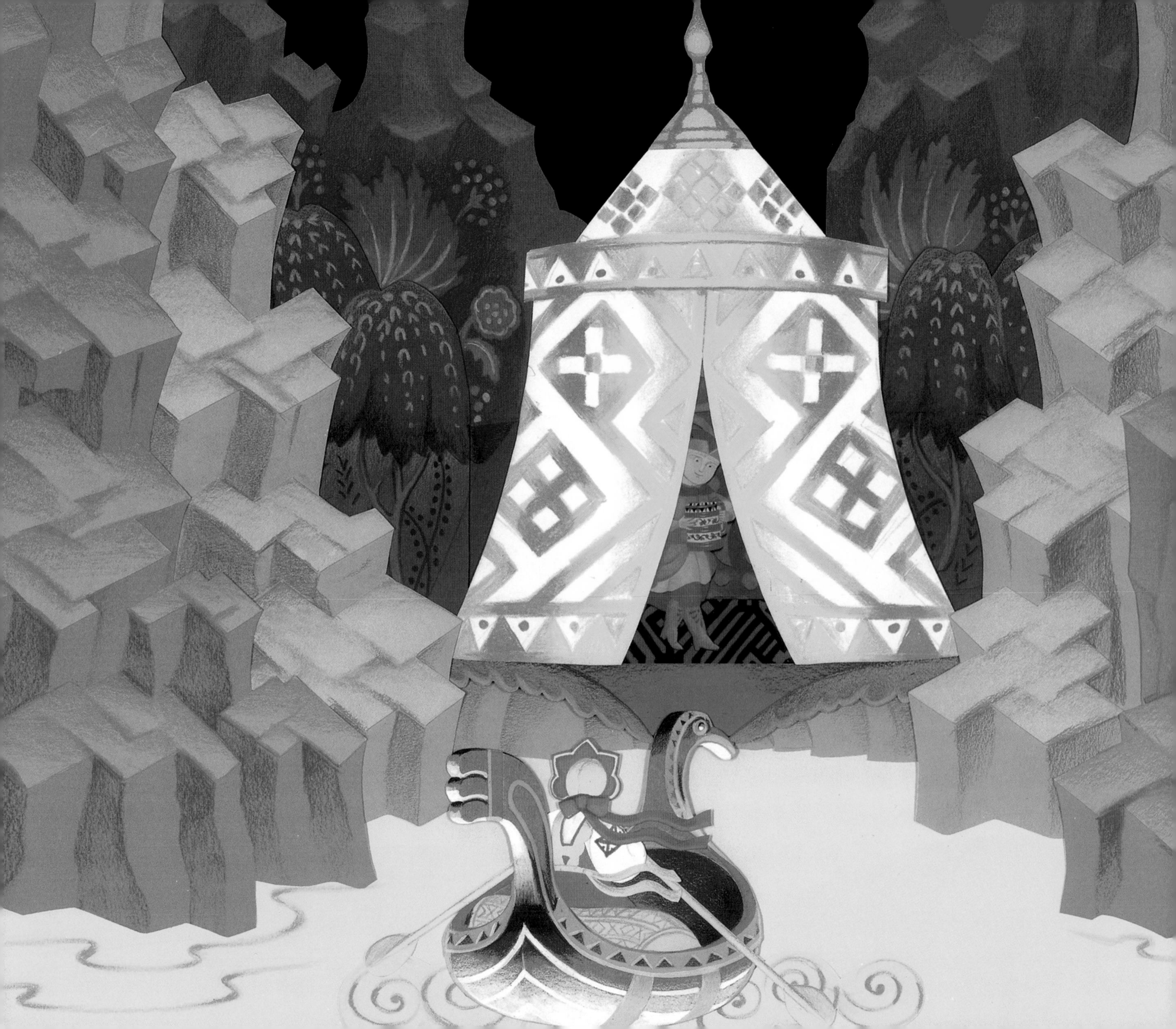

Before long the princess saw the gleaming tent onshore and smelled the exquisite food, and she grew considerably curious.

She rowed closer, cautiously, until she could see Ivan eating delicious nuggets of chocolate. She grounded her boat, crept onshore, and, when she peeked inside the tent, she, too, was quite taken with the young archer.

"Good afternoon, fair Princess," Ivan said. "Be so good as to lunch with me. As you see, there is plenty."

The princess sat and shyly tasted some sweetmeats. Their attraction quickly grew into love as the two of them talked about everything there was to talk about. But no sooner had the princess drunk some wine and the first droplet trickled down her throat than her eyelids grew heavy and she fell fast asleep. If she had been beautiful before, she was lovelier still when she lay in that deep sleep.

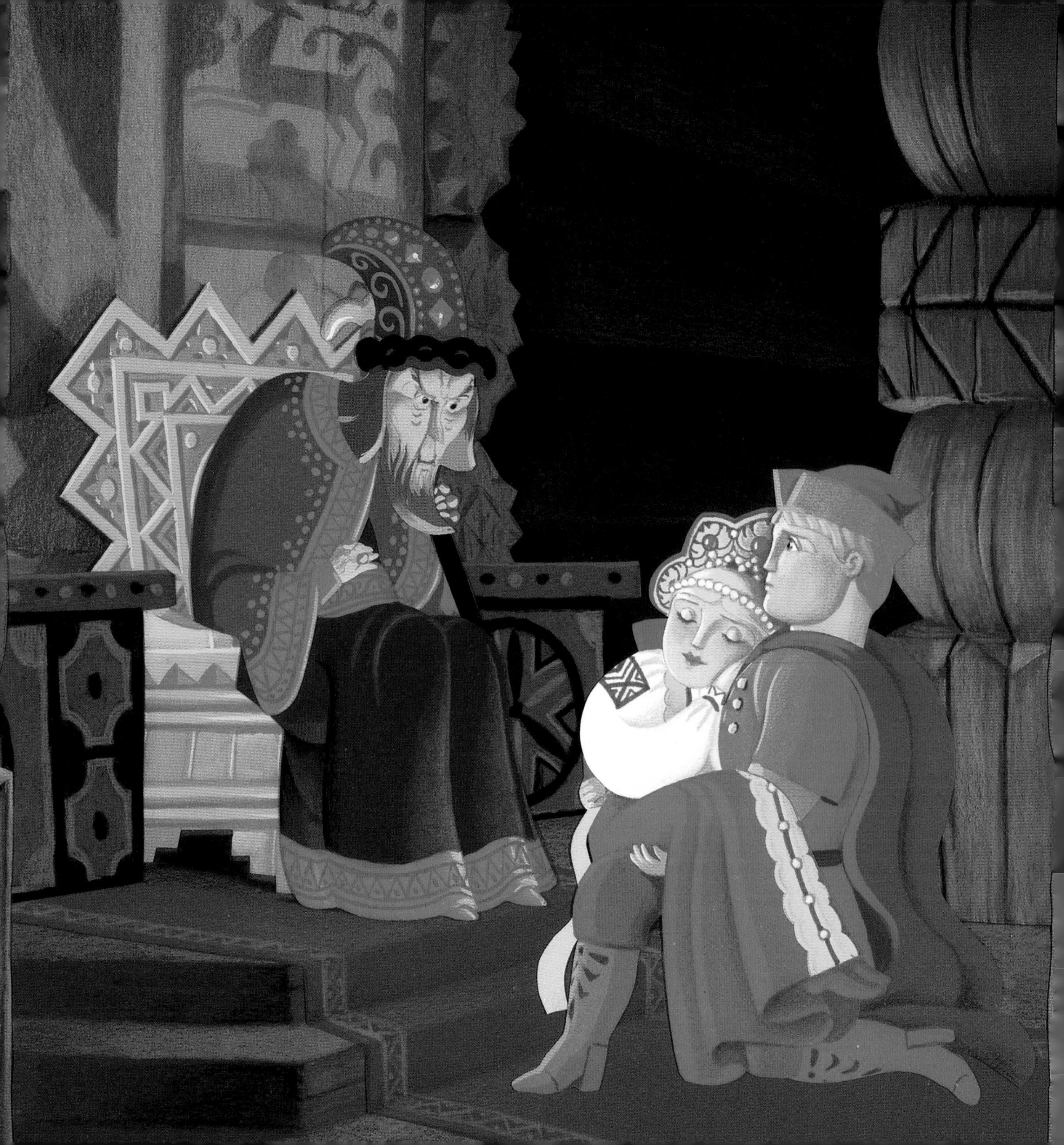

Ivan gently cradled her in his arms and mounted his horse, and together, quickly, the three of them thundered away from the Land of Never.

When they returned to the czar's palace, Princess Vasilisa was still fast asleep in Ivan's arms.

And when the czar saw her, he cackled with glee. "Sound the trumpets!" he screamed. "Ring the bells! Today shall be my wedding day!"

At once, the palace shook with the peals of rusted bells and the blare of ancient trumpets.

"Where am I?" Princess Vasilisa said, rubbing the sleep from her eyes. "Where's my silver boat and my sea of flames?"

"Princess," the czar laughed, "your sea is far away, and for that miserable silver boat I offer you a throne of solid gold."

The princess looked up at the czar for the first time and she gasped at the hideous man. She then cast Ivan a pleading glance, for she knew the young archer truly loved her. But there was nothing Ivan could do but keep silent and feel his heart slowly tear in two.

"I will not marry you," the princess said to the czar.

Well, the czar grew extremely angry, for he was accustomed to having exactly what he wanted in exactly the way he wanted it. So he demanded the princess explain why she wouldn't marry him.

She thought quickly and said, "I cannot be married without my wedding dress, which lies buried under a boulder deep in the sea of flames in the Land of Never."

Upon hearing this, the czar stamped his feet, pounded his fists, and pointed at Ivan. "Get the dress," he screamed, "or I will have your head chopped off!"

Again, Ivan went to his horse, and this time he wept buckets of tears, for finding the princess' dress was quite an inconceivable task. Besides, he loved the princess himself. Yet as before, the Horse of Power told Ivan that this was all the result, for good or bad, of taking the Firebird feather. And then they charged off, once again, to the Land of Never.

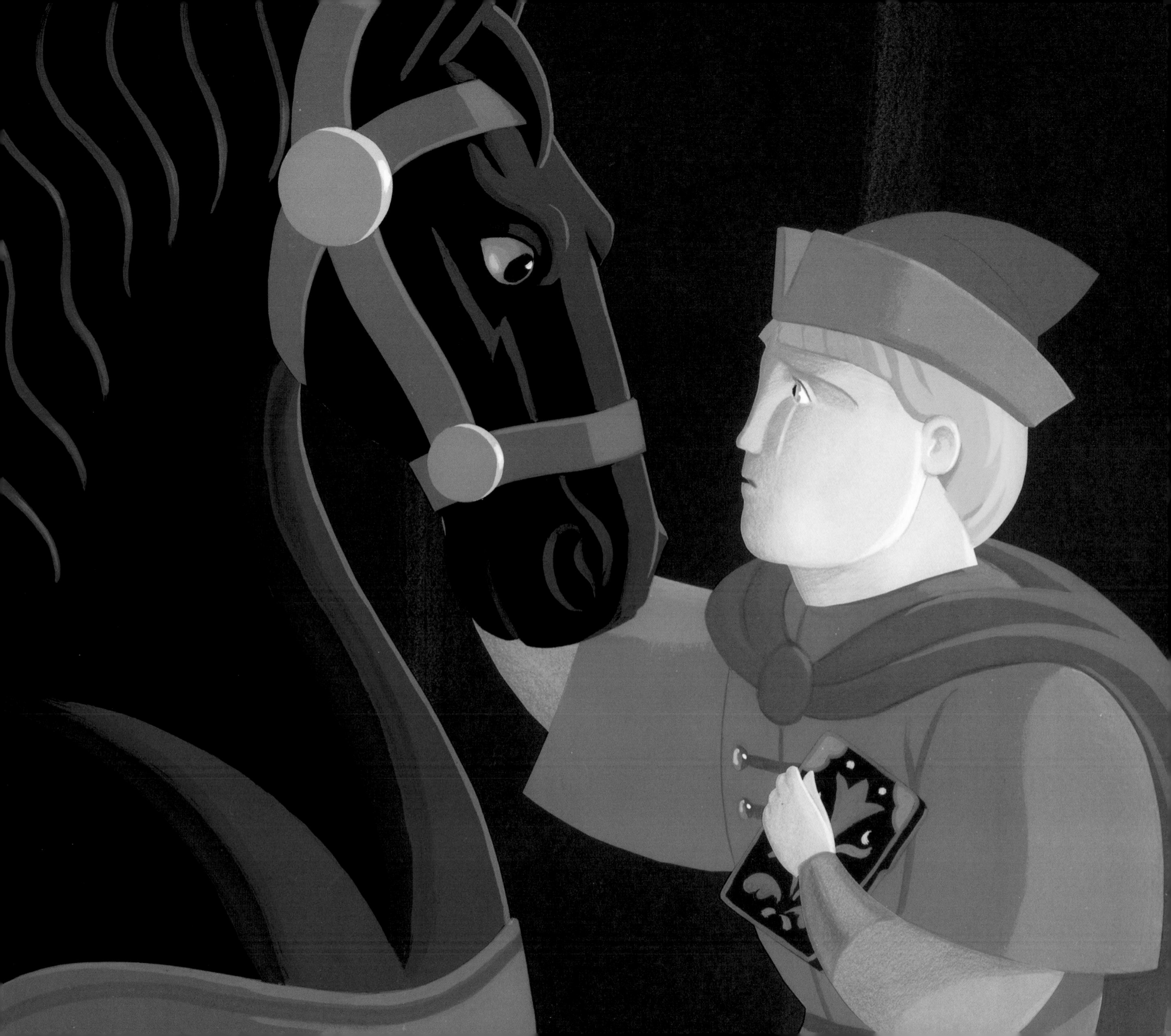

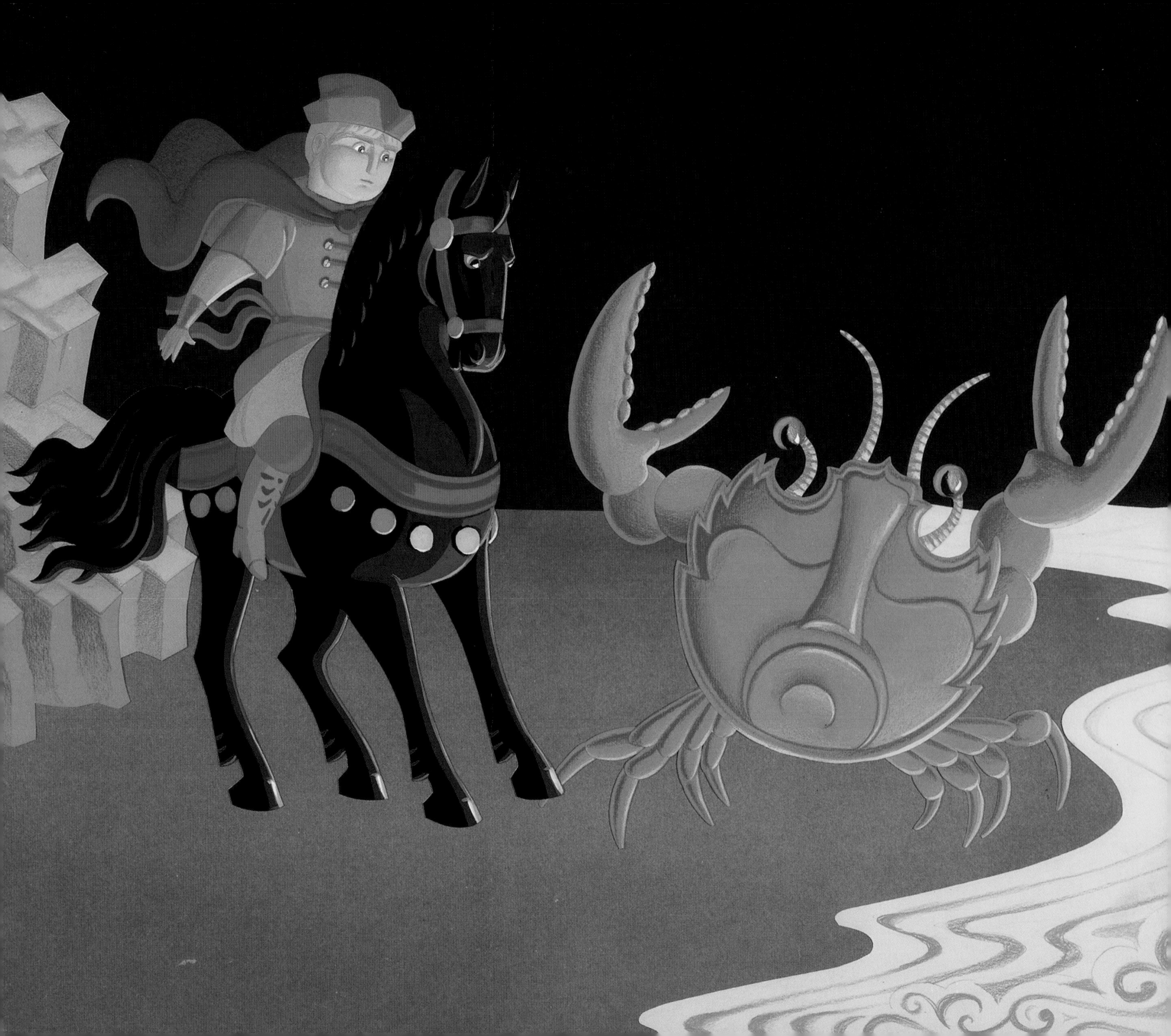

This time when they reached the sea of flames, Ivan's horse saw an enormous crab scuttling along the shore. This was the biggest crab in the world, the very czar of all crabs. It moved slowly, sideways, lumbering toward the sea. And just as it was about to shuffle back into the flaming water, the Horse of Power pinned the crab's leg with his iron hoof.

"What are you trying to do, horse?" the Crab Czar groused. "Kill me? Break my leg? Please get off!"

"Very well," the horse said. "But first you must promise to find Princess Vasilisa's wedding dress, which lies hidden under a boulder in the sea of flames."

The Crab Czar instantly agreed. He cried out in a loud cranky voice and immediately, all along the shore, thousands of smaller crabs emerged.

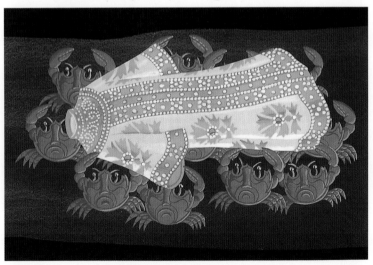

Then they all dived into the water at the Crab Czar's command.

Minutes later, they came back with the wedding dress in their claws. And Ivan thanked the crabs, grabbed the dress, and charged back to the czar's palace on his Horse of Power.

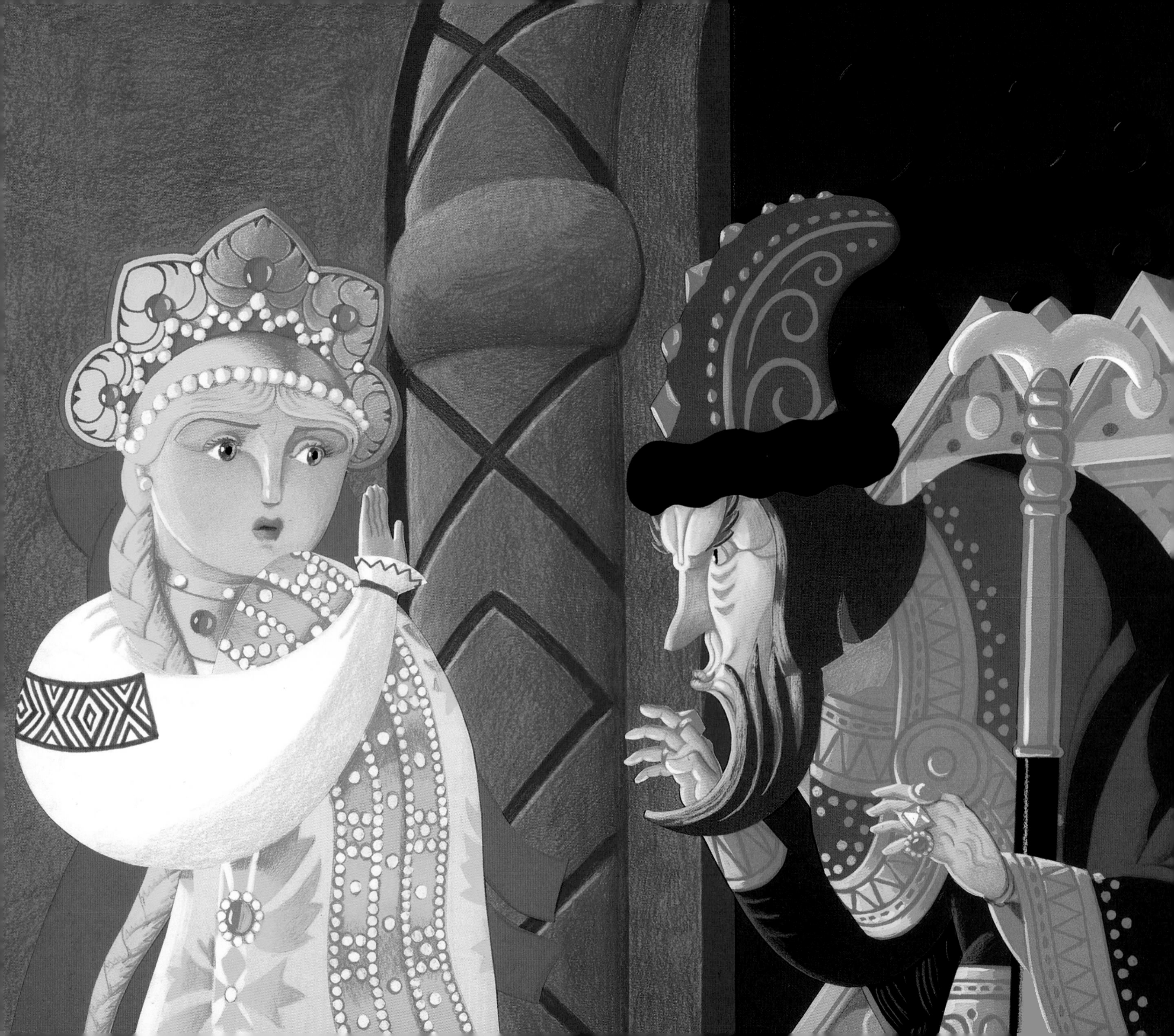

It was late in the afternoon when they returned to the kingdom. The streets were already clogged with people, curious to see the czar's new bride. And at the top of the cathedral steps, the czar had set up his throne with Princess Vasilisa next to him. She looked as bleak and sad as a Siberian night during the winter solstice. Ivan went up to the princess to give her the dress and looked at her with sadness in his eyes, and she looked at him with love.

When the czar saw Ivan with the dress, he rubbed his hands together and chuckled. "Now, my princess, we shall be married."

And he was about to kiss the princess' cheek when she held up her hand

and said, "No! We cannot be married until the young archer is burned alive in a kettle of boiling water."

Ivan's heart sank with despair at the words of the princess. Even the czar was surprised at this request. But so it must be. The czar ordered a brass cauldron filled with water and a great fire built beneath it.

As the preparations were underway, Ivan was granted one final request. He chose to bid farewell to his faithful Horse of Power, and there he wept a great Volga of tears.

"Farewell, horse of mine," he sobbed. "I should have listened to you in the first place and never taken the Firebird feather. For now I shall never know the joy of loving Princess Vasilisa. And you and I shall never again ride together through the forests. Never again, horse of mine, for I am going to be boiled alive."

And with that, Ivan hung his head and his horse nuzzled him ever so gently. "Ivan," the horse whispered. "Fear not. Trust in love. When the time comes for them to cast you in the cauldron, run and leap into it yourself."

Ivan went back to the cathedral, resigned, grieving his unfortunate fate. And though the cauldron was boiling when he returned, Princess Vasilisa announced that she herself would make sure the water was hot enough.

She peered into the cauldron and, just then, a single silver tear swelled from the corner of her eye, traveled down the length of her cheek, and dropped soundlessly into the steaming water.

Then she returned to the top of the steps, nodded to the czar and said, "Cast him into the cauldron!"

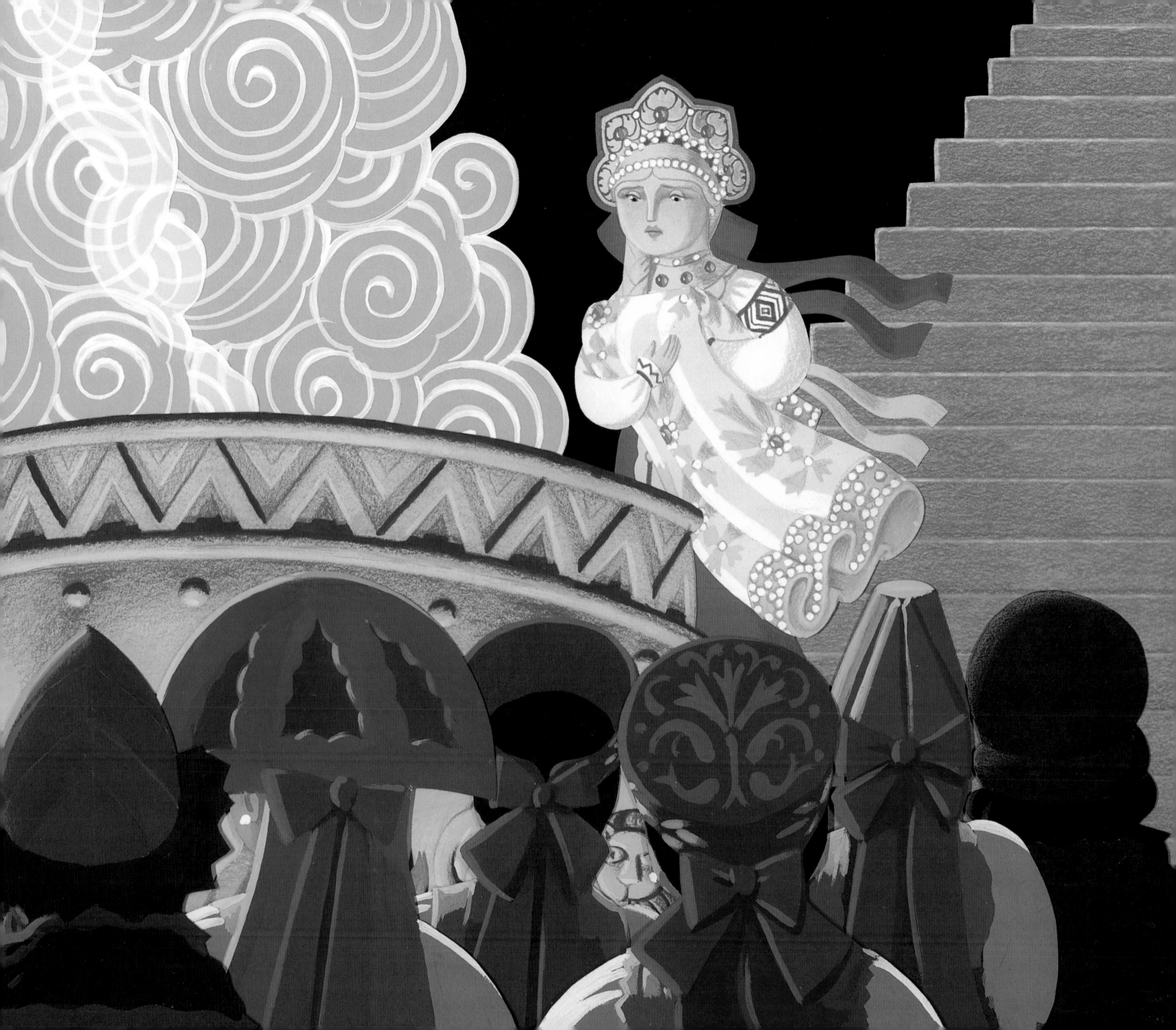

At that the crowds fell silent, and you could hear the water foam and bubble in its brass cauldron. And at that very instant, Ivan flung himself free of the guards, ran headlong down the stairs, taking four steps at a time in great hurtling leaps, and dived right into the middle of the cauldron, disappearing under the seething water.

The people elbowed and jostled to see what had happened. The czar, too, widened his eyes in curiosity. And just when they thought Ivan was cooked, he popped his head out of the water.

And then, to everyone's astonishment, Ivan climbed from the cauldron and stood transformed before them, younger and even more handsome than before, glowing golden like the Firebird herself.

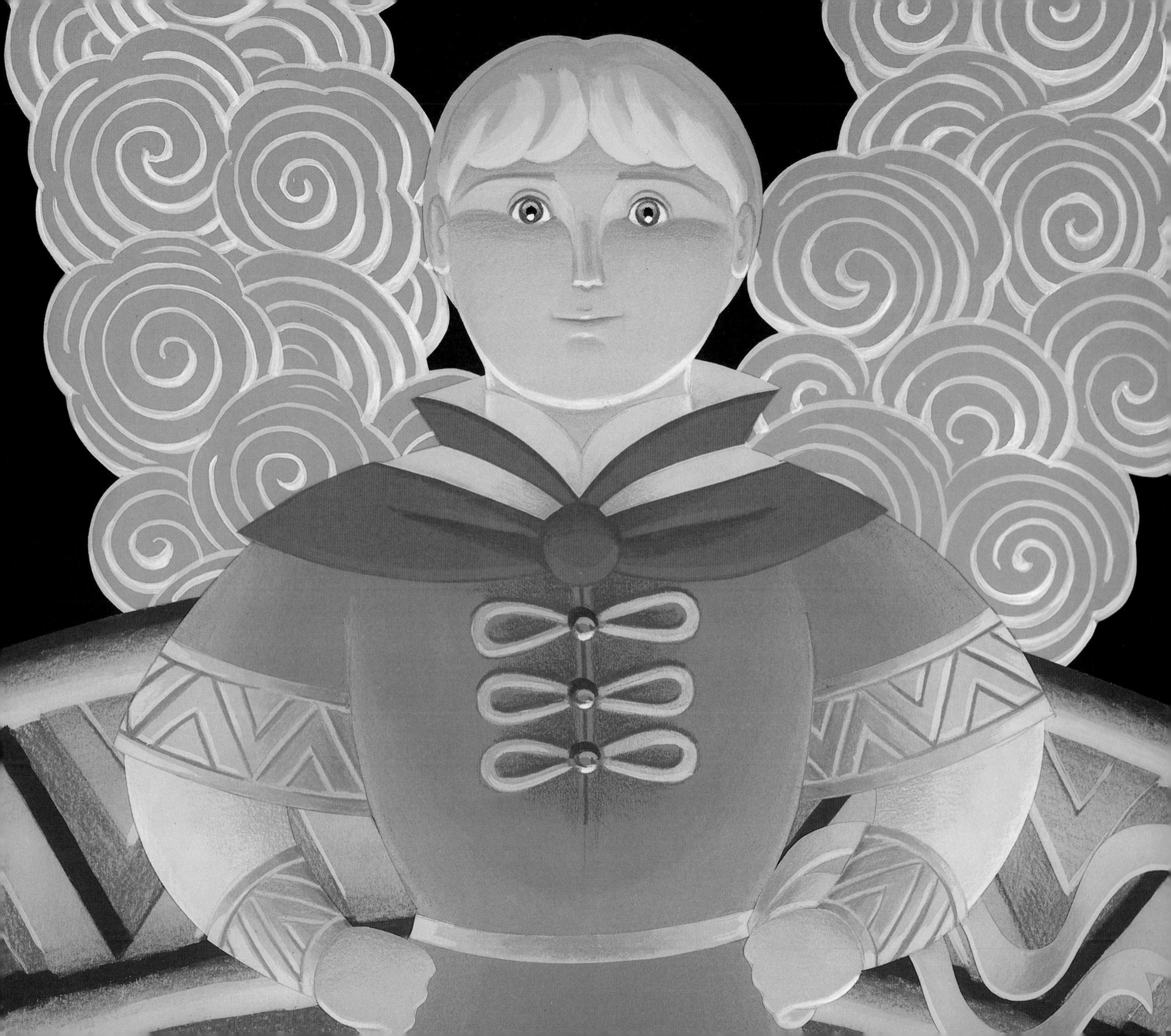

"This is a miracle," the czar proclaimed from his throne. And the czar decided that if that water could make him younger and more handsome and provide him with more years on earth with which to rule over things, he, too, wanted it.

"Make way!" he exclaimed, wobbling down the steps and clambering up to the cauldron. And the minute the old czar plopped into the water, he was boiled straight away.

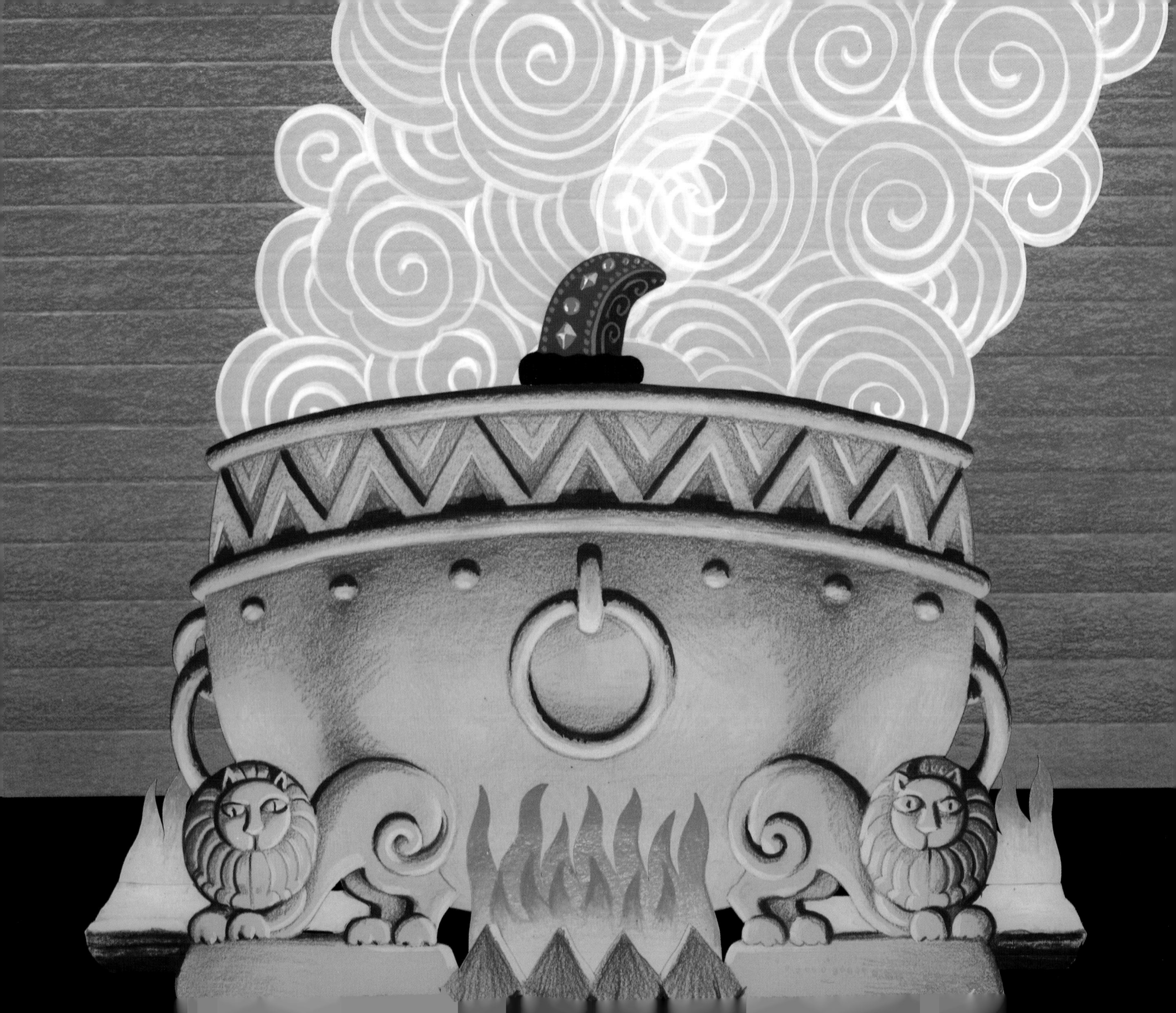

So that evening the people of the kingdom celebrated and held an enormous feast with all the czar's food and cakes and wines. Ivan and Princess Vasilisa were joyously married. And though all the people insisted they become the new czar and czarina, they both refused.

And with the Horse of Power and Princess Vasilisa, Ivan went into the palace and removed the cage where the Firebird was kept. And in front of all those rejoicing people, as the sun was setting for the night, they let the Firebird free. And she flew off, high into the evening sky, showering sparks of gold over the land, flaming gloriously.

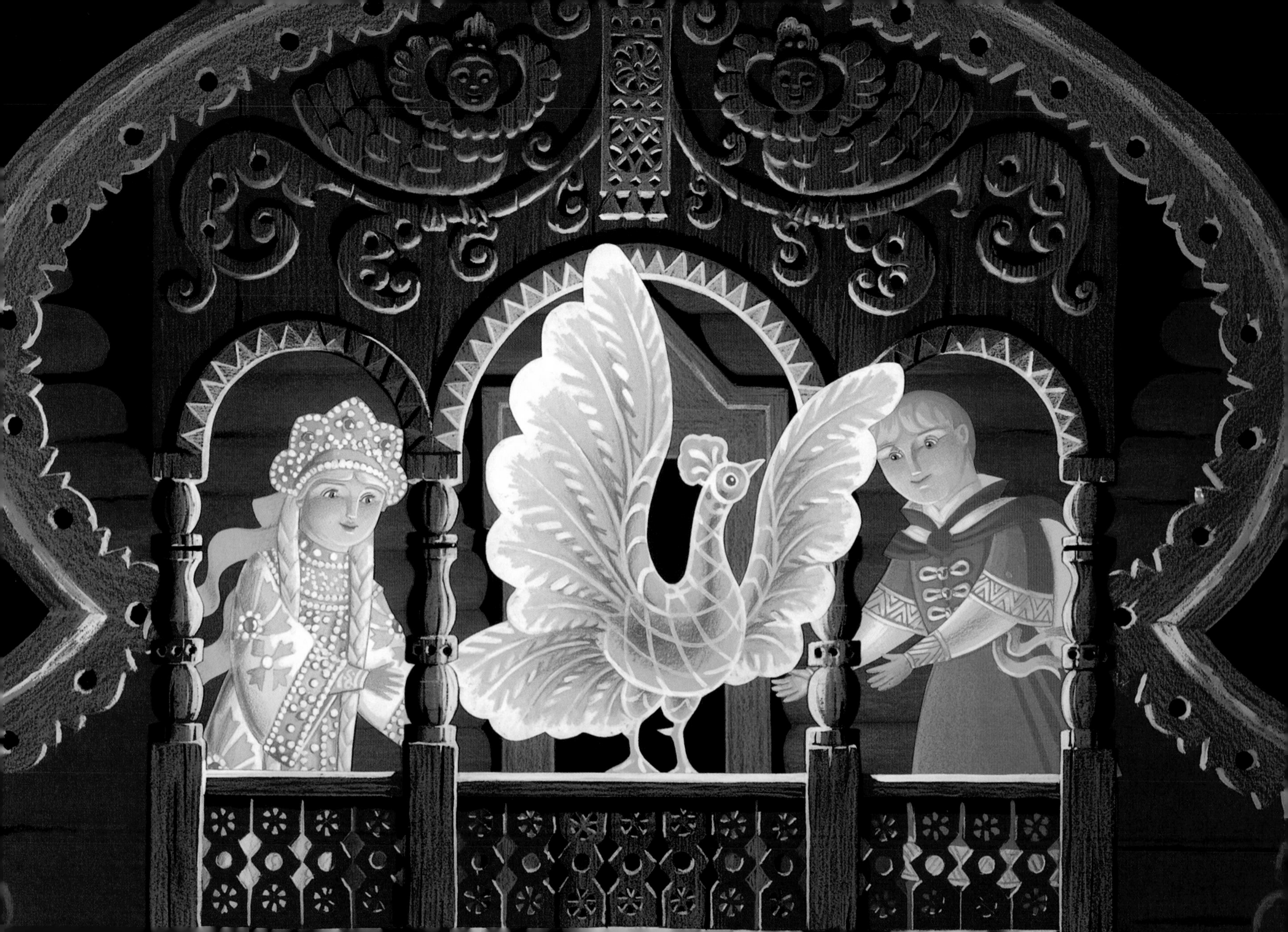